For MARGOT and ZOE

First published in Australia in 1988 by Angus & Robertson,
an imprint of HarperCollins*Publishers*

Edward the Emu
Text copyright © 1988 by Sheena Knowles
Illustrations copyright © 1988 by Rod Clement
First American edition, 1998
Printed in the United States of America. All rights reserved.
For information address HarperCollins Children's
Books, a division of HarperCollins Publishers,
195 Broadway, New York, NY 10007.

Library of Congress Cataloging-in-Publication Data
Knowles, Sheena.
    Edward the emu / Sheena Knowles ; illustrated by Rod Clement. —
1st American ed.
        p.   cm.
    Summary: Tired of being an emu, Edward decides to try being like
other animals at the zoo, but he soon discovers that being himself is
the best after all.
ISBN-10: 0-06-443499-0 (pbk.)   ISBN-13: 978-0-06-443499-7 (pbk.)
    [1. Emus—Fiction.   2. Zoo animals—Fiction.   3. Individuality—
Fiction.]   I. Clement, Rod, ill.   II. Title.
PZ7.K764Ed   1998   97-27449
[E]—dc21   CIP
                                                                 AC

16 17 18 PC 30 29 28 27 26 25 24

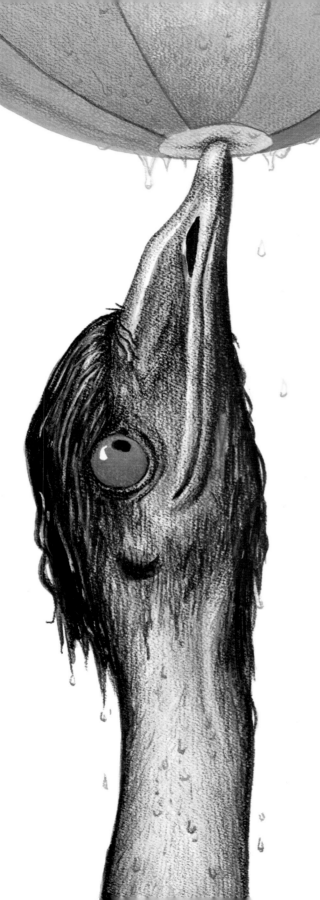

EDWARD
THE
EMU

SHEENA KNOWLES
Illustrated by
ROD CLEMENT

HarperCollins*Publishers*

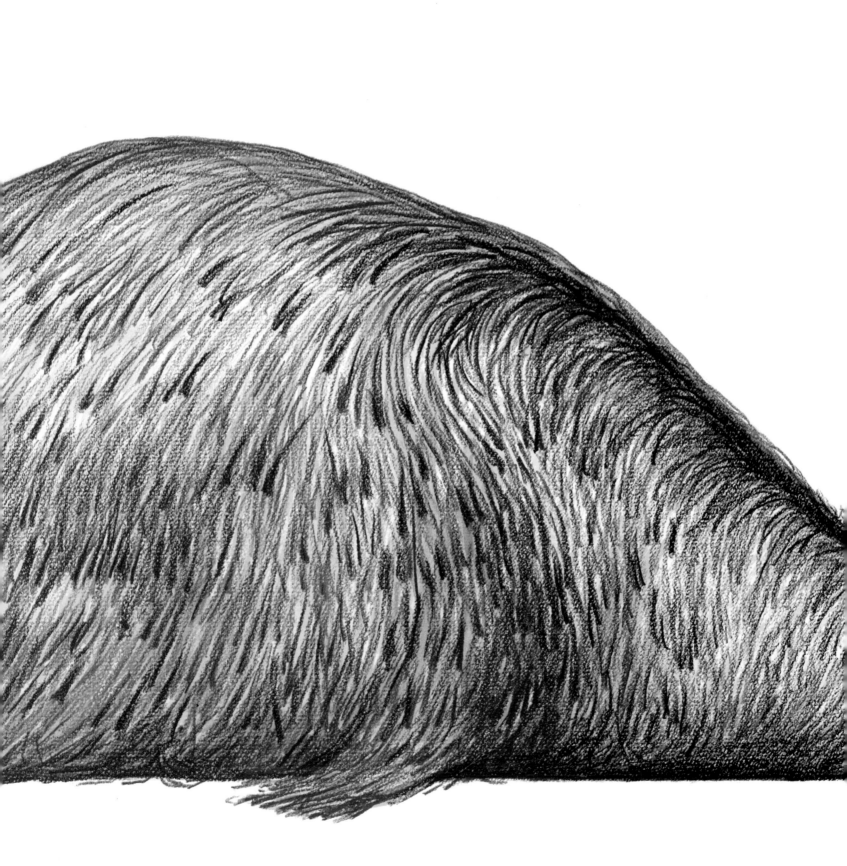

Edward the emu was sick of the zoo,
There was nowhere to go, there was nothing to do,
And compared to the seals that lived right next door,
Well being an emu was frankly a bore.

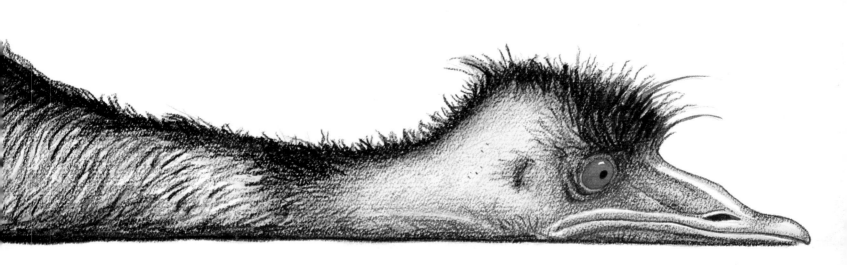

So that night when the zookeeper went home to bed,
 Edward jumped from his pen and he laughed as he said,
"The seals are best, anybody can tell,
 So tomorrow I'll just be a seal as well."

The next morning at nine when they opened the zoo,
The seals were swimming, and Edward was too.
He dived in the water and basked in the sun,
And he balanced a ball on his beak just for fun.

Well Edward was really enjoying the day,
   Till he overheard someone behind the fence say,
"The seals are always amusing, it's true,
   But the lion's the best thing to see at the zoo."

So that night when the zookeeper went home to bed,
   Edward jumped from the pool and he smiled as he said,
"The lion's the best, anybody can tell,
   So tomorrow I'll just be a lion as well."

The next morning at nine when they opened the zoo,
The lions were roaring, and Edward was too,

He snarled at the ladies and growled at the men,
Life was certainly grand for a lion in his den.

Well Edward was having a wonderful day,
Till a man in the crowd had the gumption to say,

"The lion's a beast I shall always detest,
  The snakes are the things that I like to see best."

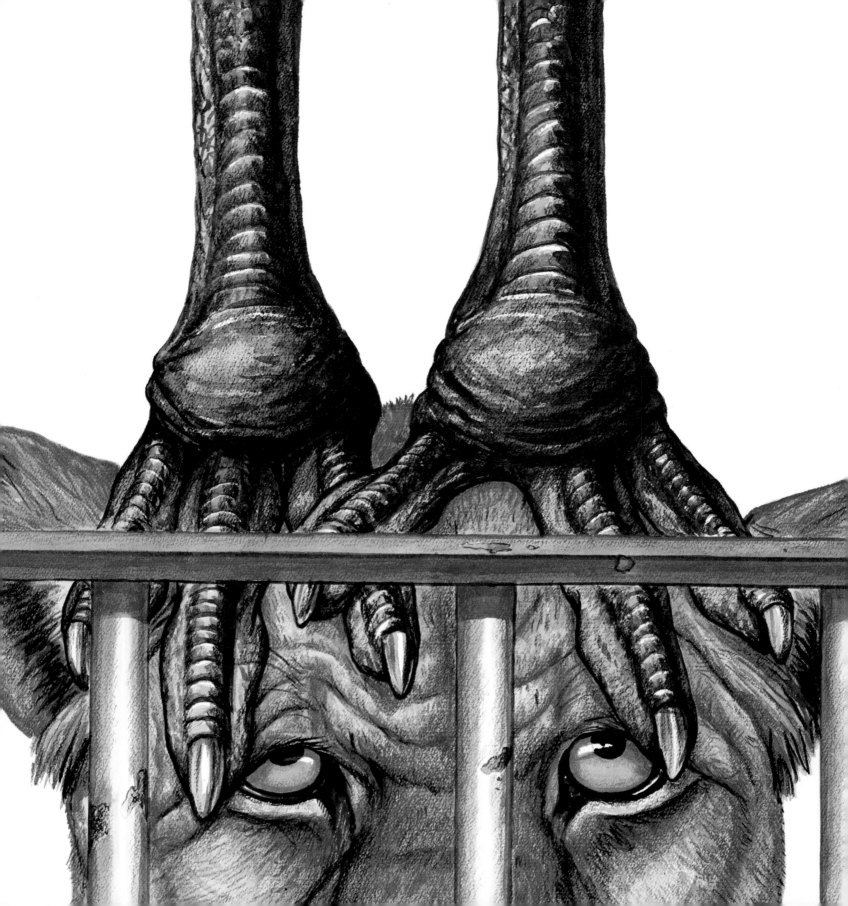

So that night when the zookeeper went home to bed,
Edward crept from the cage and he grinned as he said,
"If the snakes are the best things, and that's what they say,
Then tomorrow I'll just be a snake for the day."

The next morning at nine when they opened the zoo,
The snakes were all hissing, and Edward was too,
He slipped round the rocks, it was magic to see,
Then he curled himself casually up round a tree.

Well Edward was just warming up for the day,
When he overheard one of the visitors say,

"The snakes are impressive, I know that it's true,
But the emu's by far the best thing at the zoo."

"The emu!" gasped Edward, "My goodness that's me!
    I'm the thing that that gentleman most likes to see!
Not the seals, the lions, the snakes and the rest,
    It's Edward the emu he likes to see best!"

So that night when the zookeeper went home to bed,
Edward slipped from the cage and he laughed as he said,
"If the emu's the best, then that's easy then,
Tomorrow I'm Edward the emu again!"

Edward ran to the place where he used to reside,
But oh what a shock when he clambered inside!

He found himself suddenly come face to face,
  With the emu they'd brought in to take Edward's place!

The emus considered each other a while,
  Then the new emu said, with a shy little smile,
"Hello, I'm Edwina, it's nice meeting you,
  You're the best thing I've seen since I came to the zoo!"